DINOSAURS

igloobooks

Tommy T-Rex and Sukhi Stegosaurus are
best friends and have lots of fun together.
Can you spot them in every scene in this book?
Start by finding all the things in the picture opposite.

Tommy T-Rex   Sukhi Stegosaurus

COOL CANYON

Try to find all these things.

2 cacti

3 tumbleweeds

6 bones

DINO WORLD

Look carefully at the busy dino scene below.
Then, try to find all the items shown on the right. Don't forget
to look for Tommy T-Rex and Sukhi Stegosaurus too!

Now can you find these things too?

1 hatching egg

3 volcanoes

4 snails

7 pink plants

8 trees

10 red dragonflies

ROAR-SOME SEARCH

Tommy, Sukhi, and all their friends are exploring the shops today. Can you find the dinos and all the other items pictured below?

Now can you spot these things too?

2 shopping bags

3 green hats

4 cakes

Compsognathus Café

BARYONYX BAKERY

8 flags

9 drinks

10 purple plants

Look carefully to find all these things.

3 waterfalls

4 rounded rocks

6 green frogs

7 lily pads

8 blue leaves

10 fireflies

SPLASH LAGOON

Time to cool down and have some fun in the lovely lagoon.
See if you can see Tommy and Sukhi having a splashing good time.
Don't forget to find all the other items pictured on the left.

Try to find all these items.

2 jukeboxes

3 vinyl records

5 burgers

6 milkshakes

9 pancake stacks

9 bottles of ketchup

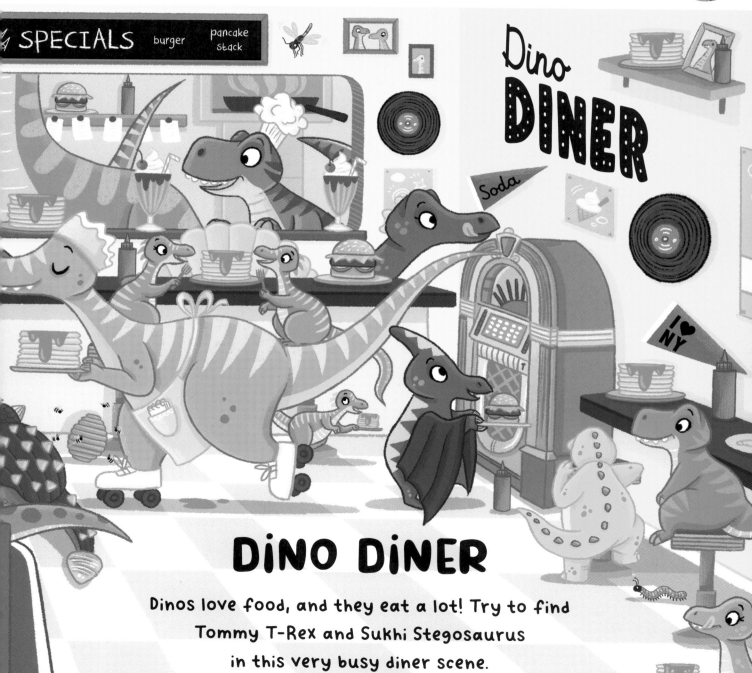

DINO DINER

Dinos love food, and they eat a lot! Try to find
Tommy T-Rex and Sukhi Stegosaurus
in this very busy diner scene.

SEA SEARCH

Lots of dinosaurs and their fishy friends live in the sea. Search this watery scene carefully and try to find Tommy and Sukhi.

Now can you find these things too?

1 duck-billed platypus

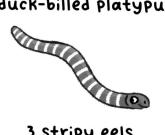

3 stripy eels

4 turtles

7 clamshells

8 rainbow corals

10 ammonites

CARNIVAL FINDS

It's time for a fun day out at the theme park.
Can you see Sukhi and Tommy enjoying
the rides and snacks?

Now can you
find these
things too?

2 rainbow lollipops

4 foam fingers

5 T-shirts

6 balloons

7 toys

10 tubs of popcorn

Try to find all the
things shown below.

2 snowmen

4 hot chocolates

5 red snowboards

6 beanie hats

7 flags

10 snowball stacks

HAVE AN ICE DAY

Search this wintry scene for Sukhi and Tommy.
There are lots of other things to spot too. Try to find
all the fun items pictured on the left.

Try to find everything shown on the right.

3 tropical islands

4 crabs

5 pieces of seaweed

7 monstera leaves

8 stripy shells

9 coconuts

FUN IN THE SUN

All the dinos love to be beside the sea in the sunny weather.
Try to find Tommy and Sukhi on this crowded beach.
Then, search for all the items pictured above.

FiELD DAY

It's time for some sporty fun! Look carefully at the scene below and try to find Sukhi and Tommy. When you have found them, look for the other items pictured on the right.

Now can you find these things too?

1 trophy

3 hurdles

4 pom-poms

5 water bottles

7 soccer balls

10 cones

FOREST HUNT

Sukhi and Tommy are hiding in this forest scene. Try to find them both. Then, search for all the items shown below.

Now can you find these things too?

2 logs

5 birds

6 mushrooms

6 beetles

10 grasshoppers

20 pine cones

WELL DONE!

You found everything so far. But how closely were you looking?
Go back through the book, and find these items in each picture too.

A pink caterpillar

A red spider

A rainbow dragonfly

A ruby

A green ladybug

A patterned egg

A beehive

A daisy

A rainbow lizard

A blue frog

BONUS ITEM!

Can you spot the gold leaf
hidden somewhere in this book?